IT'S NOT EASY
BEING A LITTLE FART

Ben Jackson & Sam Lawrence

Illustrated by Danko Herrera

Editor: Bobbi Beatty

www.indiepublishinggroup.com

Being different gives the world color.

–Nelsan Ellis

Hi! I'm the Little Fart! You might know about me from my adventures with my best friend, Timmy. If not, that's okay. I'm here to tell you all about me! Timmy and I go everywhere together, and each day is an adventure. Hockey, soccer, the dentist, and the zoo, we do it all together. We even met Santa Claus and his reindeer!

What you don't know is that I have a huge family! That's right, there is a whole heap of different Farts who are all related to me. Today, I want to introduce you to some of my relatives and tell you a little bit about my family, the Fart family. It's not easy being a Little Fart, but I wouldn't swap my family for anything!

My mom is a Silent Fart! You'll never see her coming, and no matter what you smell or hear, she'll never admit it.

My dad is a Huge Fart! When he walks into a room, everyone knows he's there, and he isn't afraid to let everyone hear him.

My brother is a Stinky Fart! It doesn't matter if he's sneaky or noisy. Whenever he shows up, you can be sure everyone is going to run out of the room!

My sister is a Squeaky Fart! She's kind of cute and adorable, but she sounds like a squeaky little mouse or a balloon with its air being let out.

My uncle is a Long Fart! He starts off quiet, but then he just seems to go on and on with a huge, noisy finish! Don't get him started, or you'll be waiting forever for him to finish!

My auntie is a Backseat Fart! Whenever you're travelling in a car or bus and smell something funny, you can guarantee it's my sneaky old auntie, Backseat Fart!

My grandpa and grandma are Old Farts! They're not like the rest of our family. They are always popping around to visit, and we get to do cool things with grandma and grandpa!

That's my whole family. There is me, the Little Fart, grandma and grandpa, the Old Farts, mom, the Silent Fart, dad the Huge Fart, my brother, the Stinky Fart, my little sister, the Squeaky Fart, my auntie, the Backseat Fart, and my uncle, the Long Fart.

We may all be different, but together, we're just one big, happy family! It's important that you love your family equally. Just because someone may be a little noisier or smellier doesn't make them bad, just different. We don't always get along, but in the end, we're family. What kind of farts are your family?

What type of farts are your family?

If you were a Fart what would you call yourself?

Note From The Authors

As Indie authors, we work hard to produce high-quality work for the enjoyment of all of our readers. If you can spare one minute just to leave a short review of our book, we would greatly appreciate it!

Let everyone know just how much you and your children enjoyed Timmy and his fart!

We are currently working on expanding this series so stay tuned for future updates by following us on Facebook or visit our website!

www.facebook.com/MyLittleFart & www.mylittlefart.com

Thank you, Ben and Sam ☺

OTHER BOOKS BY BEN & SAM

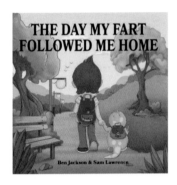

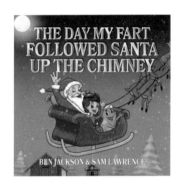

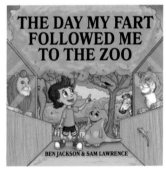

Manufactured by Amazon.ca
Bolton, ON

11257652R00017